12:02AM

Volume I

Exploring B

CICI. B

For all the women

who embrace their right

to explore,

and to be explored.

12 :02AM

.

I was 19 years old the very first time I read an erotica book. Not only did I immediately grow a love for them, but I also decided, right then and there, that one day I too would write my own erotica books.

Whether a story was a work of complete fiction, taken directly from the imagination of the author, or sprinkled with fantasies they had actually conquered at some point in their lives never mattered to me. For me, it was always about the escape. A way to explore my sexuality, privately. You may never think you'd be into something, but then you read about it, and all of a sudden, all of these desires begin awakening inside of you.

Desires, you didn't even know existed.

I always loved the thrill of it all: the anticipation, the surprises, the discoveries. And not only what I discovered about *my* desires, but also about the desires of other people.

There are so many "rules" in our day to day lives, and so many judgments when you're face to face with society talking about sex. But erotica is like sitting in front of a window, watching others, with nobody else around to influence your thoughts, and realizing that sex is different for everyone. There's more than one way to enjoy it. For me, there was always something incredibly freeing in that.

To be quite honest, erotica books were what taught me how to be comfortable with my own sexual wants and needs, to be unapologetic for them, and to not judge others for their own sexual wants and needs. Whatever two consenting adults choose to do with each other is their business. Everything isn't for everyone, and that is perfectly fucking okay.

Crave

/ krāv/

verb

feel a powerful desire for (something).

12 :02AM

Forehead to forehead,

we stare down at each other's lips.

Time has completely stopped,

and the noises from outside

no longer exist.

Our mouths slightly open,

we take turns breathing lust into one another,

like life itself.

I close my eyes, and I surrender

to your magic,

our matching vibes

and to this night.

Dear Diary,

I knew I wanted to feel him inside me from the very first moment he spoke to me. Something about his aura... it oozes sex.

His tone of voice is deep, yet soft at the same time. Whenever he speaks to me, he locks his eyes on mine and stares into them with such intensity that my body heats up instantly. Simply being in the same room as him, his mere presence, turns me the fuck on.

Every time I close my eyes, I imagine him doing things to me—good things to me, great things to me, breath-fucking-taking things to me.

I can't even help myself.

I imagine him holding my body hostage against his.

And I want that.

God, do I ever want that.

I imagine what his lips would feel like against mine, how his tongue would taste in my mouth, and what his hands would feel like gliding up and down my body.

I don't even know how the fuck this happened. It was almost out of nowhere to be honest, but the electricity between us is becoming undeniable.

A few nights ago, as we were lost in conversation, he placed one of his hands on my bare thigh. All I could think about was him moving it higher.

I wanted him all over me.

I wanted to be all over him.

I wanted to know what he sounded like when he moaned.

I wanted him to know what I sounded like,

yelling his fucking name.

"B, did you hear what I just said?" He asked. I snapped out of my dirty thoughts and blinked. "What? No, I'm sorry. I didn't." I admitted, my cheeks getting warm. "Yea, you kind of looked like you were in another world." Little did he know, the other world, was him.

I want him to know when I'm alone at night, in my bed, touching myself, I think of him and imagine that my hands, are his.

I want him to know I picture his head between my legs, and me, on the brink of cumming.

I want him to know I'm absolutely, and shamelessly fucking desperate to taste myself on his lips after my body is done convulsing and dripping into his mouth.

I want him to know it all, but I just can't bring myself to tell him, not yet.

Good Idea(s)

"B! ... B!" Angel shouted, pulling me out of my imagination, and back into reality. I turned to face her and she laughed. "The hell is wrong with you?!" I giggled, pushing my stray jet black curls away from my face. "Nothing! Nothing's wrong. I was just thinking, damn! Can't a girl have some alone time with her own friggin thoughts for a moment?"

Angel was standing in front of me, dressed in the third outfit she'd picked to try on in the store. She put her hand on her size eight hip. "If I woulda known you were gonna be zoning in and out of your own damn dick-related thoughts today, I wouldn't have asked yo' ass to come shopping with me to help me choose a damn dress. I woulda dragged Jazzy's high-fashioned self." She rolled her eyes, and I giggled some more.

"Who told you my thoughts were dick-related!? And, I liked the first one you tried on better," I said.

She turned and looked in the mirror, tilting her head to the side, as she gave herself a once-over in the navy-blue, short, strapless dress. "Really?" She asked. "But I like this one, a lot."

Jesus Christ. There was a reason why I always HATED shopping with her, and this was it! The shit was pointless. She'd ask your opinion, knowing damn well she'd already made up her mind. The shit made no sense. Fucking Leos, man.

"Then get that one then, Angel! Shit!"

She smiled at me through the mirror, flipping her long blonde weave over her shoulder. "You hate me."

"I reeealllyyyy do!" I said laughing. "You're so fucking annoying."

"And," she added. "I knew you was thinkin' about dick, 'cause you had the *I'm thinkin' bout dick* smirk spreadin' all across that pretty lil' light-skinned mouth of yours."

"Just fuck off," I told her laughing some more. "I have so many other things on my mind too."

"Like picking a dress for yourself so you can come out with your girls tonight?" She asked, batting her freshly done lashes at me.

"Yea, no." I said, and she rolled her eyes again.

The saleswoman had made her way back over to us to check on Angel. "Oh wow! This is stunning on you. The size is perfect! And it really brings out your beautiful, naturally golden skin!"

"I know, right?" Angel asked, feeling herself. I shook my head, chuckling. Only her, man, only fucking her.

. . .

"So, what the hell are you gonna do tonight then?" Angel asked, as we walked across the street from the mall to the restaurant. "I'ma stay home, just chill, and catch up on some reading."

"You're crazy," she said. "You're about to miss the party of the year, to stay home and read? *Booorrriing.*"

"Shut up, Angel."

"I'm just sayin'!" She exclaimed. "Or wait ... is 'catch up on some reading' code for, *'I have a booty call tonight that I don't wanna tell my girls about'?*"

"What? No!" I shoved her playfully. "I wish I had booty call though. Shit, I need my booty to be called, and maybe spanked, and maybe li.."

"Okay nigga, we get it." Angel said, holding up her palm to me. "Gawt damn."

We walked into the restaurant laughing our asses off, and a hostess showed us to our table. We sat, and not even a second later, a waitress came over. We wouldn't be *us* if we didn't order some type of drink to start, so we opted for a bottle of Pinot.

"Nah, but all jokes and dick-talks aside," Angel started, "Something more has *definitely* been on your mind lately. We all know when you're stressed about something, because you lock yourself up in your house, and turn inwards. Shit, just getting you out of the house today was a miracle. So, spill it. What's really going on with you, B?"

She clasped her hands together and brought them under her chin. She stared at me with concern.

"I despise the fact that y'all know me so well." I scowled after the waitress had gone. I rubbed my temples, and sighed. "I'm stressed about everything, but to start, I have some sort of stupid ass writers block, which hasn't let up for a month now. Not only is it stressing me out, it's fucking with my feelings, like, it's legit making me sad. Writing is me. I am writing. So when I'm staring at a screen, or my paper, and no words are coming out of me, I feel like shit. I feel, unlike myself. I don't know how to explain it any better than that. It just fucks me right up. Then there's work, which is actually kicking my ass. I dream of the day that I can quit that fucking job, and NEVER look back. And these bills? Girl ..." I shook my head. "It's like every time I turn around, there's something new that has to be paid."

"I feel you on the work and bills part girl, trust me," she said. "But, this book though, you been working on it for a good while now. This is the one about your life story, right?" I nodded my head. "Well," she continued, "maybe you need to put that one aside for a bit, and work on a different one." The waitress came back with our bottle, filled both our glasses, and left us with two menus.

"What do you mean?" I asked.

"Well, I mean, I don't know shit about writing, but I listen to you talk about it all the time, and I see how dedicated you are to the mere process, and this isn't the first time you've hit some kind of wall with this book, so it just makes me think, maybe this specific story isn't ready to be all the way written yet. And maybe that's why it's causing you to have these blocks or whatever." I sipped my wine as Angels words quickly began making sense. "Go on," I urged.

"Maybe there's a story inside you that needs to be told, *before* you tell that one." She took a sip from her glass and then snapped her fingers. "Like all the shit that happened between you and that good for nothing cockroach, James? Girl, that right there, is a book on its own!"

James was my ex. An ex who, let's just say, wasn't a very good guy to me.

As soon as she mentioned his name, a whirlwind of flashbacks of all he had put me through (and all I had put myself through with him) danced throughout my mind. I thought about the therapeutic letters I had written to him over the course of three years. Letters that were written during my pain and confusion about what had happened between us, to keep myself from going crazy. Letters he never read, because I never sent them. Letters that sat in a shoebox in the back of my closet. Letters that no one, not even Angel, knew I had written.

I tapped my finger nails against my glass, lost in thought. Angels idea had stirred something inside me. She may very well have been onto something.

"Judging by the look on your face and the fire I just saw in your eyes, I think you've got yourself a new book on your hands, girl." She grinned. "Lunch is on me. You can grab the next bill when that 'bestselling author' check comes through." She winked, and I smiled, still thinking about that shoebox filled with all of my truths.

Could this really be what had been blocking me?

Was the universe trying to tell me something all along?

Could I turn those letters into an actual book?

Could that be my *debut* novel?

Thinking about it, both excited and scared the shit out of me at the same time. Those letters were fucking brutal. Honesty in its entirety.

Vulnerable.

Naked.

Me.

But I couldn't shake what the idea of it had already awakened inside me. My plan to stay home that evening and catch up on some reading was still in effect. The only thing that changed was the material. That evening, I was going to pull out that shoebox, and read all of the old letters to my ex.

"Are you ladies ready to order?" The waitress asked.

"I am," I answered. I always ate the same damn thing at that restaurant. I already knew what I wanted. "And it's going to be one bill please, *on me*." I looked over at Angel. "Because my BFF is the shit."

Angel and I exchanged high fives, and our waitress smiled as we ordered our food then switched the topic of conversation and began talking about the party she and the rest of my squad were attending later on.

By the time our food came, we were pretty much done with our bottle of wine, and needless to say, I was feeling a lot more relaxed. While the thoughts of the new book idea still coated my mind, my 'dick-related thoughts' definitely hadn't strayed too far either.

I thought about *him*—the one I had been craving.

Maybe the night would turn into something more than reading after all. Maybe, instead of waiting for *my* booty to be called, I would pick up the phone, and do the calling.

Maybe ...

Orgasm

/ˈôrˌɡazəm/

noun

a climax of sexual excitement, characterized by feelings of pleasure centered in the genitals and (in men) experienced as an accompaniment to ejaculation.

12 :02AM

I've been dancing with the thought

of giving you a taste.

Your face, buried between my legs.

Your tongue, lost in the middle of my secret place.

Your hands, wrapped firmly around my thighs.

Pleasure moans escaping my lips.

My hands, caressing the back of your head,

while I slowly rock my hips.

My body, burning with pleasure

feeling myself about to release.

You holding me, steady, as you whisper

"that's right baby, cum for me."

Over the edge, losing all control,

as I let the waves of my nectar flood freely.

Shaking, begging, and screaming your name,

You drinking every drop, and then smiling

as you look up at me . . .

Yes, I've been dancing with the thought

of giving you a taste.

So keep your phone close,

'cause you might just get that text

It will read, simply—

"Meet me after midnight. 12:02AM, at my place."

Dear Diary,

Would it be too forward of me to tell him I want him just for tonight? Would he be thrown off by a woman like me, who knows exactly what she wants?

I don't want him to be my boyfriend. I don't want one of those right now. I've got too much going on, and the "boyfriend" shit just doesn't fit into my life plans right now. Sue me.

Someone at work the other day told me I had commitment issues—which is totally fucking false. God, I love when people try to diagnose you with a condition that you don't have, all because the way you choose to live your life at the moment, is the polar opposite of the way they're living theirs. "You're in denial," she had the nerve to follow up with. I wanted to punch her right in the damn throat.

Just because you and every other woman around you has a boyfriend, wants a boyfriend, needs a boyfriend, can't fucking breathe without a fucking boyfriend— doesn't mean there's something wrong with the one woman in the room, who doesn't want, or isn't looking for that. What a far-fetched thought it must be, that maybe, my desires differ from yours. Jesus.

Anyway, fuck her.

Right now, my only want, is for him, to satisfy my needs... just for tonight.

Too forward or not, I'm about to let him know.

Uninterrupted Ecstasy

It had been a long time since I had felt the type of chemistry I felt with him, with anyone. We laid in my bed silently pressed together. Me, in an oversized t-shirt and panties, him in his undershirt and boxers. With his huge arms wrapped around me, he held me tightly and exhaled.

His body was warm, calm, and incredibly comforting.

I felt so tiny in his arms. I *was* so tiny in his arms, and I loved it. My face pressed into the top of his chest. I kissed it, closed my eyes, and I too exhaled.

I felt safe.

I felt fucking good.

You know how they say cuddling can reduce stress, and even relieve pain? Well, whoever "they" are, aren't lying. My whole body was relaxed. My mind was at ease. The pain in my shoulders I had been walking around with for the last couple of months, was gone. He was the complete opposite of anything I was used to. There was nothing complex about him. There was nothing aggressive about him. I wasn't confused about him, nor did I question myself around him.

He was, especially in this very moment, my peace.

He kissed my forehead, and I looked up at him. I couldn't stop smiling. He opened his eyes and smiled back. Inching my face closer to his, I kissed his lips, and when I felt his tongue slip into my mouth, my heart began to race. My body came to life all on its own.

We laid there, wrapped in each other, taking turns as we held each other's lips hostage, enjoying every moment of it. The electricity between us was undeniable as he kissed me and gently caressed the small of my back at the same time. I in turn, caressed his face and neck. Nothing about being with him felt wrong—nothing—and my panties were way too fucking wet to stay on.

He was what I had been craving after all, and I needed him. I needed him right then and there.

I bit the bottom of his lip gently and held it with my teeth as I ran my hand from his neck, down his smooth chest, right to his waistline and tugged at his boxers. He understood my language. And without taking his lips away from mine, gingerly, he pushed me onto my back, putting himself in control. I immediately submitted to him, willingly.

Spreading my thighs apart with one hand, he placed his body between them. I exhaled deeply, my body aching with anticipation. He took his lips away from me, and I opened my eyes, staring at him on his knees between my thighs. He pulled me forward into a sitting position and began lifting my shirt. I raised my arms to help him pull it off me and he locked his eyes on my gaze. I helped to take off his shirt too. His skin was the color of midnight magic—beautiful. Hungrily, I leaned in and kissed all over his chest, as he once again gently pushed me onto my back.

I didn't resist.

He took his time as he kissed me everywhere—soft, sweet, wet kisses. He moved from my mouth, to my neck, down to my navel. I felt like he was kissing away every problem I had ever had in my life. Every single time I felt his lips connect with my body, it was as if I was being healed. He erased my memory, and replaced it with that sole moment. I couldn't remember anything before him. I couldn't think of anything else, other than the moment I was in.

Serenity in my mind and excitement rippling through my body, I bit my bottom lip, held onto the sheets, and closed my eyes. I surrendered to his touch. I moaned as he made his way back up to my breasts, took one in his mouth, and sucked it gently. I thought I was going to explode on the spot. He was teasing me, forcing my senses to be caught in between not wanting him to stop what he was doing, and wanting him to put himself inside me as soon as possible.

I didn't know which one I wanted more.

But as he left my breasts and moved his mouth down between my legs, pushed my panties aside with his teeth, and began to work his tongue over the most sensitive part of my middle, there was no more confusion.

I needed him to stay.

Right.

Fucking.

There.

He started lightly and very slowly, almost tickling the top of my clit. But the louder my moans became, the quicker the flicks of his tongue became. Little by little, he added more pressure. Then I reached down with my hands, placed them on the back of his head and managed to let out the words, "Oh my God, stay *riiight* there!"

I wanted to hold back because it felt *soooo* good, but I couldn't fucking take it anymore. With my eyes still closed, and hands, now completely locked onto the back of his head, I didn't even have the time to tell him

I was cumming. I squeezed my thighs against his cheeks as I felt the waves of my orgasm surge through me; and the more I came, the steadier he was as he licked every last drop of my nectar.

I couldn't breathe. My body trembled with raw, uninterrupted ecstasy, and as I slowly came down from my high, he took his tongue away. He kissed my body, making his way back up to my mouth. I opened my eyes and watched him. He was *soooo* fucking sexy, and I couldn't wait to taste my own juices on his lips. "Kiss me," I whispered to him. He immediately obliged to my demand, and as he did, I felt his hardness throbbing as it rested on top of my pussy. I spread my legs wider in excitement—ready, and needing to feel all of him inside me. But before he filled me up, I wanted to taste him first. I moved my arms beneath his chest as it rested on top of mine. I pushed him, gingerly.

"My turn," I purred.

He positioned himself on his back, and I climbed on top of him. He reached up, grabbing the nape of my neck, bringing my head down to his level and kissed me some more. There was so much passion between us. I swear, I never knew this much passion between two people was even possible. I finally managed to pull myself away from his lips. I started to make my way down between his legs. With one hand stretched across his chest, I held his thickness in the other. Slowly, I began running my tongue over it from the bottom to the top. It was my turn to tease him.

I went back and forth between using just my tongue, and stroking him with my hand. He was stirring and moaning, and the mixture of both was driving me crazy in all the right ways. I was enjoying being in control of his pleasure. He called out my name, and I gazed up at him, "Fuck, you're amazing," he whispered. I smiled naughtily. Then, I made sure his eyes were locked on mine. I wanted him to watch as I took his entire length into my mouth, slowly, and as far down my throat as it could go.

I watched him as he threw his head back, exhaled, and submitted to delectation.

I kept my pace slow and steady at first, paying close attention to the movement of his body and his sounds. In that moment, it was all about him. I wanted to take him to a place he had never been before, the same way he had taken me. Making him feel good, was making me feel good, and the more excited he got, the more excited I got.

It was a win-win situation.

He was rock hard in my mouth, and I began to pick up my pace. His whole body was warm, and he had begun moaning just enough to let me know that he might explode at any minute. But I couldn't let that happen, not just yet. I needed to feel him inside of me first.

Kissing my way back up to his neck, I climbed back on top of him, and without warning, lowered myself onto his hardness. My pussy was already dripping, and he slid right in—the most perfect fit I had ever had.

Our bodies instantly connected sensations, and right away, our breathing became in sync.

We held onto each other, as he thrusted from beneath me and I rocked on top of him. Keeping my face buried in his neck, I sucked on the side of it as hard as I could, trying to keep myself from screaming out every curse word imaginable.

Without separating himself from me, he tenderly flipped me onto my back. I loved every moment of how our bodies effortlessly communicated with each other.

Placing my two hands on the bed, over my head while interlocking his hands with mine, he brought his lips back to my lips, and then pushed himself deeper inside me.

The length of him made me moan pure pleasure into his mouth. The deeper he pushed, the harder he kissed me, and the harder he kissed me, the tighter I squeezed his hands.

I felt the waves inside me. They were on their way again, and I held onto him for dear fucking life as they came.

Feeling my walls tense up, gripping him, he knew exactly what was on the way. He groaned— "Cum for me B. Cum for me."

And I did exactly that.

My body temperature was at an all-time high as I dug my nails into his back, squeezed my thighs against his waist and let myself fucking go. He rode my waves with me until he felt them calm, and then it was his turn. Speeding up his thrusts, all the while keeping his lips pressed onto mine, I felt his body jerk as he quickly pulled himself out of me and released onto my inner thigh.

He collapsed beside me, taking me into his arms.

Our hearts were racing. We were out of breath. As he held me, all I could think about was how fucking perfect I felt. My craving for a night of uninterrupted ecstasy, had been satisfied.

Suck

/sək/

verb

draw into the mouth by contracting the muscles of the lip
and mouth to make a partial vacuum

12 :02AM

I got you.

Lay on your back, stay still, and close your eyes,

not because I don't want you to look at me

but because,

I want you focused

on the way my tongue feels on you as it glides.

I want you to relish in this moment.

so I'm gonna suck, and lick all over you,

real slow.

You're gonna feel what you've been missing,

a reminder, of why you never wanna let me go.

I've missed you too though, I've needed you.

I've yearned for this moment right here.

And all of the things that you love to hear me say,

I'll be sure to whisper, softly, into your ear.

Tonight is for you.

I know you've had a long, and hectic day.

So relax,

keep those eyes closed

and let me take all of your stresses away...

I got you.

Dear Diary,

There's just something about taking the man I yearn for, into my mouth... hearing him moan with gratification. Watching him sink deep into bliss. A bliss I created, for him. A bliss that I enjoy creating for him.

There's just something about taking the man I yearn for, into my mouth...giving, while I take. It just makes me...

come alive.

Crimson-Coloured Passion Marks

Tiny wisps of hair began caressing the parameter of my forehead. The steam from the shower forced them to break free from the bun that sat tightly on top of my head. The lukewarm water cascading down my back was soothing. I lathered the front of my body with coconut scented suds, humming along to the sound of Sade's mellow voice singing "The Sweetest Taboo" through my surround sound.

I closed my eyes, and thought about *him.*

We were both entrepreneurs, constantly occupied with our businesses. Our schedules rarely permitted us to see each other as much as we wanted. Regular people with regular lives, planned evenings together—but we weren't regular people, and our lives were far from regular. Most of the time, we'd have to steal evenings together; tonight was one of those nights.

He had messaged me around 10PM, asking what I was up to. It just so happened that I had finally wrapped up the last chapter of my book. I was attaching it in an email to my editor when the text came through.

I smiled at his impeccable timing.

"I was actually getting ready to pour myself a glass of Pinot, to celebrate me finally finishing the book," I texted. *"Care to join me?"*

"I'm proud of you," he texted back. *"And yes, joining you is something that I need right now."*

"Come through," I responded.

"Be there in about an hour," he replied.

Placing my phone back on my desk, I sat back in my chair and sighed. "It's about to be two perfect endings tonight," I said to myself out loud.

I closed my laptop, and stretched my arms above my head.

Though we both lead very demanding lives, I knew this past week in his, had been more overloaded than usual. He had a lot on his plate, and was the type of person who never asked for help (which reminded me a lot of myself). He never complained about his workload though. He could be stressed as fuck, but if anyone were to ask him how his day was going, his answer would always be "It's going great." But I wasn't just anyone, I always knew better.

I shook my head, smiling, thinking about his pride. I rinsed my body free of soap and decided, that night was going to be for him. Yes, I had something to celebrate. But he had something he needed, more than I needed to celebrate. He needed to escape. He needed to relax. He needed to drown in something other than work—and I was going to provide the perfect pool for that.

Stepping out of the shower, I dried myself with the towel. I scanned the variety of lotions on my counter top, trying to decide which scent I wanted to envelope myself in for the evening. I opted for the Victoria's

Secret 'Blush', which combined the scents of grapefruit blossom and magnolia.

After smoothing it over my skin, I threw on a black, knee-length, silk robe. I reached up and freed my curls from the elastic they were trapped in, letting them fall to my shoulders.

My phone chirped on the table. *"10 minutes,"* the text read, and I felt my pussy tingle with delight. *"The door's unlocked,"* I wrote back.

Swiftly, I glided from room to room, lighting four candles in each. Then I grabbed the bottle of wine from the cabinet, filled two glasses, and set them on the coffee table in the living room. I sank comfortably into my sofa, and waited.

Fifteen minutes later, my front door opened and I smiled, a naughty smile.

The smell of his cologne immediately filled the air as he walked in, took off his shoes, and made his way toward the sofa.

"Damn, B," he said, towering over me.

"Good evening, Sir." I cooed, patting the vacant space next to me. "Sit."

He obliged, and I handed him his glass of wine.

"You look, and smell like something I wanna taste," he said.

"Oh, don't you worry. I'ma feed you later."

I sipped my wine and eyed him as he took a sip of his. He laid his head back and sighed. I leaned over and softly kissed his cheek. He closed his eyes. "Mmmm," he let out, reaching for my thigh with his free hand. "Hey," he whispered suddenly as he opened his eyes turning to look at me. "I'm extremely proud you." I blushed and looked down. "Thank you," I said. "No, seriously." He moved his hand from my thigh up to my chin, forcing me to look at him. "I've never known another woman who works the way you do. I've never watched another woman in action, dedicate herself to her dreams the way you have. You're the most stubborn woman I have ever met in my entire fucking life, and Lord knows, sometimes it makes you quite the

fucking handful," I giggled, and he continued. "But
that same stubbornness is what keeps those passionate
fires burning inside you. That's what makes you go
hard for everything you want to get and achieve. That's
what sees you through every finish line you envision
yourself crossing. I can't lie, not only is it sexy, and
attractive as fuck, it's also extremely inspiring."

Damn it. He was making my pussy wet and my heart
melt at the same damn time.

"Thank you," I repeated, both flattered and humbled.

"Come here," he demanded.

"No." I refused, shaking my head, while grinning
mischievously.

I took a long sip of my wine, set the glass back on the
table, and stood.

"I'm not the only one in this room that works hard," I
said. I backed up a bit so he could see all of me.

"We can celebrate me another night. But right now,
something tells me you're the one who needs to be
taken care of.

Keeping my eyes locked on his, I opened my robe and let it fall to the floor, exposing my naked curves. "You want this?" I asked teasingly. I watched as he licked his lips, admiring me from top to bottom, devouring me with his eyes. "No," he answered. "I *need* that."

I drifted towards him slowly and got on my knees between his legs. The bulge in his sweat pants was bold and unapologetic. I glided my hand over it, massaging it gently. He exhaled deeply, letting his left arm fall to his side. I relished in knowing that he was relaxed, and comfortable. "Keep sipping," I purred.

Smoothing my hand away from his bulge, I replaced it with my mouth—kissing, lightly nibbling and sucking on it, until I felt like he had been teased enough. Swiftly, I reached inside his pants, pulled out that beautiful dick of his, and sucked it into the very back of my throat. I heard him gasp with pleasure, and the sound of it excited me even more.

I worked my magic—sucking slow but intensely at first, stroking him in between. Then I switched my pace and began consuming him, greedily, and shamelessly, until I heard him utter the words, "I need to fucking eat you."

A devilish grin spread across my lips as I licked his rock-fucking-hard dick from bottom to top one last time before rising to my feet. I took the glass of wine from his right hand and sipped before setting it down on the table behind me.

"Take your clothes off," I ordered, and he obeyed immediately. The lighting from the candles danced softly across his deep, chocolate-colored skin. Excitement fluttered through all of my senses as I watched. He was fucking beautiful.

"Lay on your back," was my next order. Once again, hesitation on his part was nonexistent.

Across the sofa, he stretched out. Climbing on top of him, I positioned my legs on both sides of his chest. I slid my pussy across it until it was sitting underneath his chin. I brought two fingers to my mouth, licked them, and then ran them up and down my already dripping wet clit as he watched.

"Eat," was my final command.

I felt his hands cup my plump ass from behind as he lifted his head a little and began to feast. I elongated my arms behind me, gripped his legs for balance and arched my back. I closed my eyes and moaned. He alternated between brushing his tongue in circles over my clit, flicking his tongue up and down, and lightly sucking it, while periodically whispering things like "You taste so fucking good B." "I love eating you." "I can't wait till you explode so I can drink every last fucking drop of you."

He was driving me absolutely crazy—the *good* kind of crazy. He knew exactly how to take me where I needed to be. Within a matter of minutes, my legs began to shake. I screamed his name as my orgasm seeped out of me and into his mouth. "Mmmmm," I heard him say, as he passionately drank from my pussy.

"Fuck!" I shouted, trying to catch my breath. Before I could say anything else, he was lifting me in his arms as he rose, placing me on my feet. Holding me tight, he brought his lips to mine. We stood kissing and groping each other feverishly, until he decided he was ready to fill me up, completely.

He spun me around, bent me over the sofa and slid inside of me, hitting the depth of my walls. Moan after moan after pleasure-filled moan escaped both our lips, and echoed throughout the entire room. "Fuuuuck," he let out, as he thrusted in and out of me from behind. "You're so fucking wet, B." I pushed my ass back against him, roughly. "Ahh fuuucck!" He cried out, and I knew he was going to cum at any moment. "You're the one that makes me this fucking wet," I told him.

With his chest pressed against my back and his arms wrapped around me from underneath, he began sucking and biting the side of my neck. He pushed harder and deeper inside of me. I clutched the top of the sofa and delightfully let him take me however he wanted to have me.

"Fuck, B."

"Cum for me my love."

"Fuck, I'm gonna cu..."

And just like that, he had pulled out, expelling his warm liquid onto my ass cheek.

I giggled as I let myself fall onto the sofa, and he kissed me on my cheek before disappearing into the bathroom.

He came back with a wet rag and gingerly wiped his mess off of my ass, then threw it on the floor and nestled beside me.

"You're somethin' else, you know that?"

Smiling, I nodded my head. "Depends on the day."

"Shit," he said, tracing the side of my neck with his finger. I frowned, knowing exactly what he was probably looking at. "What'd I tell you about sucking on my damn skin like that? I'm too light for all that shit. Hickeys aren't cute."

"Oh, but you sure as hell like how it feels when I'm givin' em to you though." He laughed, kissing the side of my neck.

"You right," I admitted. "I love how it feels."

"And I love how *you* feel." Those were the last words I heard him say before he peacefully drifted off, into a deep sleep—sleep he more than needed.

• • •

I kissed the tip of his nose, and whispered softly, "You deserved tonight." Then I closed my eyes, and fell into a deep sleep of my own.

The night was definitely for him, but he made sure I got everything I needed too.

Pleasure

/ˈpleZHər/

noun

a feeling of happy satisfaction and enjoyment.

I thought about you today

and I had to squeeze my thighs together.

Flashbacks of the way you made me feel that night,

I remember wanting it to last forever.

The sounds that escaped your lips,

as you thrusted in and out of me

were so sexy.

The way you gripped my ass cheeks from underneath
me

while you worked my middle

so gently.

There's something about you

that I can't ever seem to get enough of.

Maybe it's the way you look up at me from between
my thighs

right before I'm about to cum.

Or maybe it's the way you, effortlessly,

make my entire body

submit to you.

I become yours, instantly,

my juices now your honey dew.

I thought about you today

and I had to squeeze my thighs together.

I'm at the point where I don't want anyone else.

I just want to be yours, forever.

Dear Diary,

Nothing turns me on more than a man who enjoys exploring my body just as much as he enjoys letting me explore his. I guess sex is different for everyone— boring sex to one person, may be the best sex in the fucking world to another and vice versa.

*Personally, I think sex is special. But not in the **"make sure that you only do it with someone you love"** type of way. I mean, sure, sex is always amazing with someone you love, but, it can be just as amazing with someone you simply lust for.*

Sexual chemistry is what makes sex special to me. It's what allows you to be free with the person you're about to have sex with. In the past, whenever I was too shy to have sex with the lights on, or too shy to stare into the eyes of a man while his dick was in my mouth, or felt shy in any type of way at all, it was because the chemistry wasn't right. Now that I'm older, I get that. Plus, I'm so in tune with my body now that I refuse to have sex, just to have sex. Fuck that.

It has to be mind-blowing, every single time.

The whole point of sex, is to be completely immersed in fucking pleasure. It's supposed to make you feel like you're fucking levitating. It's supposed to bring a whole other side of you out—a hungry, shameless, sexy, confident fucking sex goddess. I'm just saying...

If you're too shy to let that sex goddess out to roam freely in the place that is essentially a dedicated zone for her to be free in, then what's the point of having sex?

What's the point of having sex with a person who makes you too shy to unleash your fucking sex goddess? I don't know man. To each their own, but I personally refuse. Not into what I'm into? That's cool—no sex. If I'm not into what you're into, that's cool too—no sex.

At the end of the day, it's gotta be mutual, and organic.

So no chemistry, no sex.

The fucking end.

In The Vault

"He said he had never licked, kissed, or even put his nose anywhere near a pussy before," I told my girls as I drove. Jazzy and Erika giggled from the back seat, while Angel, who was riding shotgun gasped.

"You're not serious!"

"Dead ass," I answered. "Yo, what do these dudes think this is!?" She screeched. "Ain't nobody got time for boring ass sex. I'm sorry, but I ain't here for the shortchanging. We need some head the same way they need some head! Shit."

"Give, and thou shalt receive!!" Jazzy and Erika yelled, dying of laughter. "Amen!" I shouted.

"Anyway, so what did you say?" Angel asked. "'Cause we all know you got your rules." I nodded in agreement. "I definitely do have my rules," I said. "And

I told him straight up that I respect his stance, but I can't even entertain the thought of being with someone who's not about that life, 'cause I AM about that life, all day. So... yeah." I felt my girls staring at me. "Well! What did he say?!" Angel asked, smirking. "I mean, we're still kicking, ain't we?" I replied as I winked.

"Ah shiiieeet," my girls sang. "I don't know how you do it," Erika said.

"Do what?"

"Get guys to basically do whatever you want them to!"

I shook my head. "Now you know that's a damn lie! I definitely don't get guys to do whatever I want them to. Shit, if that was the case, I wouldn't have spent so many years in the heartbreak hotel."

"Truuue," Angel said. "But, you for sure have a way when it comes to sex. You make sure you're gonna get yours the way you need to get yours."

I thought for a quick second. "I guess you can say that. I don't know. I mean, y'all over here making it sound like I'm forcing dudes into pleasing me *my* way," I laughed. "It's more like, I let 'em know what I need, and either they can make that shit happen, or they can't. And if they can't, well, bye boo!"

"Shit, I know my black ass ain't mad at you." Erika said.

"My black ass neither," Jazzy agreed, slapping Erika a high-five.

"Lemme ask y'all something," Angel said. "And everyone has to promise to keep it real. Bet?"

"Bet." We all answered.

"Okay, cool," Angel said. "Soooo, y'all ever been with another woman before?"

"Hell NO!" Jazzy shouted. "Absolutely fucking not," Erika confirmed.

"Okay don't be so fucking dramatic back there," Angel said, rolling her eyes. "Damn, why you getting so offended?" I asked her. "I'm not!" She snapped defensively. I laughed. "You just did it again," I pointed out.

"You never even answered the question, B." She fired back.

I tapped my nails on the steering wheel and smiled. "What the fuck?" Jazzy sprung up and gripped the back of my seat. "You taking way too long to answer the damn question, B. You fucked a girl and didn't tell us?!" Now I was really laughing. "Y'all are so fucking extra!" I said. "Shit."

"Answer the damn question, B." Angel said, smirking. "We bet on keeping it reeeaal."

"Alright," I said. "Chill the fuck out. So, I have experimented with a woman before, yes."

"THIS BITCH!" Jazzy yelled.

"Well would you look at that? You think you know someone," Erika said.

Angel smacked me on the arm. "When the hell was this? And why didn't we know?!"

"Gawt damn it. Am I not allowed to keep *anything* to myself?"

"Hell nah!!" My girls sang, and we all started laughing together. I shook my head. "It was a long ass fucking time ago, way before I knew y'all. I was probably like 19-20 at the time. It wasn't that serious."

"Well tell us what happened. Shit! Did you like it?" Erika pressed.

"Obviously if I liked it, I'd be fucking women right now instead of men. Don't you think?"

I pulled up in front of Jazzy's place, and put my hazard lights on. Angel stared at me. "What?" I asked. "I don't know why you put them hazards on, as if this convo is done and we hoppin' out the whip," she said. "You better park up! This convo is far from done." I burst out laughing as my girls in the back yelled, "Preeeaach!!"

Angel lit a cigarette as I pulled the car around to the other side of the street and parked. "Light me one too," I said. And she did. "So yoooo," Jazzy started. "What was it like? Did y'all eat each other out and shit?"

"You're an idiot," Erika said, chuckling. "What? I'm curious!" Jazzy snapped at her.

"Y'all are like two fucking children back there," I told them shaking my head. "It was legit not as serious as y'all are making it out to be. I was young. I was curious. It was like, process of elimination. How you supposed to know if you don't like something, if you never try it?"

"Did you cum?" Jazzy asked.

I took a pull from my cigarette and exhaled the smoke out of the window. "Not even," I answered honestly. "Keepin' it real—it was awkward as hell. I think I already knew that I wasn't going to like it as soon as she kissed me, but I rolled with it for a bit just to see, you know, if I was gonna warm up to the experience. But yea, nah, it never happened. I wasn't excited at all. Feeling her breasts against mine, smelling her sweet perfume instead of a manly cologne. Her tiny hands gliding up and down my body, instead of big strong manly hands—nah. I knew right away that just wasn't my thing."

"You're something else, B." Erika said.

"Why?" I laughed.

"Because! I swear you're like a vault. Got all these fucking secrets inside you, just chillin'."

"I meaaan, no one ever asked! I don't understand humans. What am I supposed to do? Just walk around blurting out random shit I've done in my life at random times, just because? Nah. You ask me something, as my home girl, I'll tell you. If we're talking about something, I may add to the convo about that specific something if I fucking feel like it should be added. Know what I mean? I just don't think I need to walk around like a fucking billboard with *aaallll* of my past experiences on blast 24/7. And, why the hell are y'all so uptight about this topic?! Jesus. Loosen up a little bit. It's not 1847 around here. Don't be so damn closed-minded."

I was starting to get a little defensive myself. I mean, so I had an experience with a woman, like 9 years ago. Honestly, who gives a fuck? And even if it was last fucking night—again—who gives a fuck? In this day and age, I don't understand why people still get all riled up about women being with women and men being with men. WHO CARES!? Everything ain't for everyone. Live your life and have sex with who you want. Let other people fucking live and have sex with who they want.

"I'm just taken aback because, well, it's you," Jazzy said. "Like, I would have never thought, in a million years, that you'd had an experience with a woman, just because you're so, like, into men—like, *real* men. You know? Like, you're the girl who thoroughly enjoys the complete essence of a man—from his courting, to his ambitions, his gentlemanliness, to his capabilities of providing for his family, right down to the smell of his cologne, like you mentioned. As modern, and independent of a woman as you are on so many different levels, you also have certain traditional qualities that you stand for. So, it's hard to picture you, you know, on the other side. That's all."

I took a second to let her words sink in, and my defenses came down. From that perspective, I could understand where she was coming from, and she was very right about me and how much I loved a real man.

"You're 100% right," I told her. "But I stand for those qualities because of my experience, and I stand for them in my own life. That's what I like. That's what I enjoy. But I don't look at other people who enjoy the opposite of what I do strangely, or as anything less than. For instance, if you came to me tomorrow and told me, "B, I'm gay," or "I'm bi." I'd be like, "Word? Didn't see that coming, and as long as you don't try to be pushing yourself up on me, I'm cool."

See, I'm cool with whatever people want to do if it makes them happy, as long as they aren't hurting themselves, or purposely hurting anyone else. Feel me?"

"Definitely," she responded.

"Same," Erika said.

I looked over at Angel, who was quiet. "What'chu over there thinking about?" I asked her. "Nothing. Just listening to you, and taking it all in. Can't even lie, I was just as shocked as Jazzy, but nah, everything you said made perfect sense."

I took the last pull from my cigarette, then flicked it out of the window and clapped my hands together. "Well alright then. Great talk heffas. Now get the hell out of my car so I can drop Angel home and carry on about my business!" Laughter rang through my car as Jazzy and Erika opened their doors and stepped out, "Alright, alright!" Erika walked over to the driver's side and bent down next to my open window. "Y'all sure you don't wanna come with us to Devon's thing tonight? It's gonna be *pooppiiin*"

Both Angel and I shook our heads.

"Nah," I said. "I've got a meeting downtown at 8AM, and I've gotta be on my A-game."

Erika looked over at Angel. "Nope," she said. "I already told y'all, if I see Devon's little bitch ass girlfriend, and she even so much as looks in my direction, I'ma fuck her up. So I'd rather keep my ass away from all of that." Erika and I exchanged eye rolls.

Devon was a dude we had all known for a while, and was damn near like a little brother to us. But word around town was that his new girlfriend was a gold-digger and using the fuck out of him. We had all tried to talk some sense into him, but he was in love. And

you know what happens when someone is in love
right? You can't tell them shit.

Angel wanted to bust her ass every time she saw her
though. So yea, it was in everyone's best interest that
she didn't go to a function that featured the girlfriend
and access to alcohol.

"Alright then," Erika said. "Drive safe hoes!" Jazzy
yelled and smiled as we pulled off.

"They're a trip," Angel said as we turned the corner.
"All day," I agreed. "Gotta love 'em."

Fifteen minutes later, we were in front of Angel's place.
"Yo B," she said. "Can I talk to you about something?"

"Always," I answered. "What's good?"

"There was a reason why I asked that question, earlier.
You know, about ever being with another woman," she
started. "Granted, I wasn't expecting *you* to answer the
way you did, but, I'm fucking glad you did. I wanted to
talk about this as a group, but I think the way everyone
else responded just threw me off. I did get offended.

You smelled it." I chuckled. "Yea, 'cause I know you!"
She smiled.

"So listen. Can I tell you something, and not have you
judge me? Can you keep it in your vault?"

*Shit. What the fuck am I about to get ready to hear
now?*

I held up my pinky finger towards her. "No judgement,
and I'll vault it." She firmly wrapped her pinky finger
around mine. "Alright," she said taking a deep breath.
"Might as well shut the car off and light up another
cig', 'cause, let's just say, it's a story. And I've gotta tell
it from beginning to end, without leaving anything
out."

Damn it. Angel was making it seem like I needed to
brace the entire fuck outta myself for whatever story
she was about to tell. I cut my engine, lit up a cigarette
and handed her the lighter so she could light one for
herself as well. I leaned back in my seat and braced
myself.

"You fucked a girl?" I asked.

"Kinda," she said.

"What do you mean, 'kinda'? You either did, or you didn't."

She sighed, a heavy sigh.

"It's complicated, B. And you know, if we were Sex and the City, I'd definitely be Samantha in this bitch. But I don't think I ever seen an episode where Samantha did what I did the other night."

Lawd Jesus. What kind of freaky ass shit did Angel get herself into?

"Alright, well, I'm listening," I said. "The vault is open and ready to receive."

She took a pull from her cigarette and smirked. "May God forgive me, because I have sinned like a muthafucka."

12:02AM

12:02AM

... to be continued

12 :02AM

12 :02AM

12:02AM

INSTAGRAM-FACEBOOK-TWITTER @THECRIMSONKISS